NEW HOPE

For Susan Pearson

Inquiries should be addressed to
Lothrop, Lee & Shepard Books, a division of William Morrow & Company, Inc.,
1350 Avenue of the Americas, New York, New York 10019.
Printed in the United States of America.
First Edition   1 2 3 4 5 6 7 8 9 10
Library of Congress Cataloging in Publication Data was not
available in time for the publication of this book, but can
be obtained from the Library of Congress.   *New Hope*.
ISBN 0-688-13925-6. ISBN 0-688-13926-4 (lib.bdg.).
Library of Congress Catalog Card Number 94-78939.

The illustrations in this book were done in.acrylics on watercolor paper.
The display type was set in Playbill and Clarendon. The text was set in Galliard.
Printed and bound by Berryville Graphics. Production supervision by Linda Palladino.

NEW HOPE

HENRI SORENSEN

Lothrop, Lee & Shepard Books   New York

JIMMY LOVED TO VISIT GRANDPA. He loved the old-fashioned ice-cream store in New Hope, where Grandpa lived. He loved the recycling dump. And he especially loved the statue in the park. "Who is that man?" Jimmy always asked. And every time, Grandpa told him the same wonderful story.

"That's Lars Jensen," Grandpa began. "Over one hundred years ago, in 1885, Lars sailed to this country from Denmark. He brought his wife, Karen, and their two children, Peter and Mathilde, to start a new life in America.

"When they landed in New York, they took a train to Minnesota. There Lars bought a wagon, two horses, a hunting rifle, tools, a tent, several bags of seeds, and plenty of food for the trip. Then he and Karen and Peter and Mathilde began the last part of their long journey. On narrow trails, they traveled through forests and forded rivers and crossed the wide plains.

"Sometimes they joined up with other travelers and Peter and Mathilde fell asleep to tales of Sitting Bull told around the campfire. One night a yellow dog appeared at the campsite. 'He must have followed us from the town we passed through this morning,' said Karen. 'Well, we can't take him back now,' said Lars. So Peter and Mathilde adopted him. They named him Fido.

"One day, just as they came to a river, one of the axles on their wagon broke. Lars took off his hat and scratched his head. Fish were jumping in the river. A doe and her fawn stood at the edge of the forest. *Pokkers!*' said Lars. 'This looks like a good place. Let's stop here.'

"By the time the first snow fell, they had planted and harvested their first crop and built a small cabin for themselves and a shed for their horses. Each morning after checking their traps, Lars and Peter worked on the fence until Karen called them in for hot stew and bread.

"The following spring, while Karen and Mathilde worked in the garden, Lars and Peter built a small ferry. All that summer Lars ferried people and wagons across the river. Business was brisk—Lars's ferry was the only way to cross the river for miles.

"One day a blacksmith named Franz arrived. A busy ferry landing would bring lots of business, so instead of crossing the river, he stayed to build a forge.

"Soon lumbermen arrived to harvest the rich forests and farmers began to clear the land for their crops. 'All these people need a general store,' said Lars, so he traveled several days to the nearest big town to buy rope and shoes and nails and fabric and all the other things he knew the people would need. He named his shop the New Hope General Store.

"As the years passed, more and more people came to the village by the river. The old slow-moving ferry was replaced by a wooden bridge. Now that crossing the river was so easy, the stage coach began to stop at the New Hope General Store. One day a traveler named Saul got off the stage and stayed. Three months later he opened the New Hope Hotel.

"New Hope became a busy, bustling place. A wagon builder set up shop next door to the general store. Then came a bank and a stable and a barbershop and a newspaper office. The *New Hope Gazette* printed all the news and invitations and signs too. Soon Main Street had shops on both sides and a church with a bell in its steeple at the north end.

"In 1900, Mathilde married Franz's son Heinrich in that very church, and the whole town came to celebrate the wedding. Mathilde and Heinrich moved into a house on the brand-new street of Maple Lane, and Heinrich built the New Hope Tannery to make the best leather gloves and saddles and boots west of the Appalachian Mountains.

"By 1910, when Mathilde's little boy, Hans, was four years old, the railroad had come to New Hope. On it came traveling actors and salesmen and businessmen and friends and some people who stayed and became new citizens."

"And then what, Grandpa?" Jimmy asked.
"And then came me," said Grandpa. "Hans grew up
to be my daddy and your great-grandpa."

"Tell about the statue," said Jimmy.

"When I was five years old," said Grandpa, "New Hope built this statue, and your great-grandpa told me the story that I just told you. It's a statue of Lars Jensen—your great-great-great-grandfather—who started this town because his axle broke."